THE
DINOSAUR
EGGS

Francis Mosley

NEW YORK

First edition for the United States
published 1988 by Barron's Educational Series, Inc

First published in 1988 by André Deutsch Limited
London, England

All inquiries should be addressed to:
Barron's Educational Series, Inc.
250 Wireless Boulevard
Hauppauge, NY 11788

Library of Congress Cataloging-in-Publication Data

Mosley, Francis.
    The dinosaur eggs.

    Summary: A lonely couple wishing for children hatches
three dinosaur eggs and raises the resulting beasts to
create an unusual but successful family.

    [1. Dinosaurs – Fiction]   I. Title.
PZ7.M8496Di 1988 [E]   87–17419
ISBN 0–8120–5910–7

Printed in Belgium

89   987654321

Alfred and Mary Watkins would have been completely happy but for one regret. They did not have any children.

One day, when he was taking his usual walk along the beach, Alfred found three enormous eggs.

He took them home and asked his chickens to try and hatch them.
After three days nothing had happened . . .

. . . but on the fourth day the eggs suddenly cracked open and three very strange heads popped out.
"Dinosaurs," cried Alfred.
The baby dinosaurs blinked, then began to howl.
Alfred carried them into the kitchen.

"They must be hungry," said Mary. "I'll warm some milk for them."
The howling stopped.

Alfred and Mary wrapped the dinosaurs carefully in a blanket and put them in a basket close to the fire. Then they settled down to enjoy their new family.

After three weeks on milk Mary thought they might be ready for
some solid food.
But what do dinosaurs like to eat?
She thought for a while, and then opened a can of cat food and gave it
to Alfred.

Dorothy the cat didn't think much of this, but the dinosaurs were so friendly she couldn't be cross for long.

Time passed and the babies grew into children,

very LARGE children,

but children nonetheless.

They had to be bathed . . .

. . . and have a bedtime story, just like other children.

They went to school like other children,

and played games like other children,

but grew very much bigger than other children.
They even grew too big for their house, and . . .

Alfred had to make a few changes.
This made them much more comfortable at home but outside there
were other problems.

The neighbors grew less friendly as the dinosaurs grew bigger. They blocked the whole road when they went for a walk, and were not always careful where they put their feet.

One day one of the dinosaurs saw some children roller skating.

It looked like so much fun he thought he'd try it himself,

but he had a bad accident.

The police arrived soon afterwards and told Alfred that he would have to take the dinosaurs away. This made them all very sad.

"Perhaps the zoo will look after you," suggested Mary. But the zoo said they didn't have enough room.

So Alfred and Mary decided to move to the country, where there would be no neighbors to upset.

They found just the right house for their big family.

It needed painting and a good cleaning, so the dinosaurs got to work.

When it was finished, they had a serious talk and decided that Mary and Alfred had given them a very happy childhood and now it was their turn to look after *them*.

So the next morning they gave Alfred and Mary breakfast in bed. Alfred still did most of the cooking, but the dinosaurs took over all the shopping and cleaning.

In this way the family lived happily together.